MARVEL
GUARDIANS OF THE GALAXY

ULTIMATE STICKER COLLECTION

HOW TO USE THIS BOOK

Read the captions, then find the
sticker that best fits the space.

(Hint: check the sticker labels for clues!)

•

Don't forget that your stickers can be stuck
down and peeled off again.

•

There are lots of awesome extra stickers
for creating your own Super Hero
adventures throughout the book.

DK | Penguin
Random
House

Edited by Cefn Ridout
Written by Nick Jones
Designed by Clive Savage and Bullpen Productions
Jacket designed by Clive Savage

First published in Great Britain in 2017 by
Dorling Kindersley Limited
80 Strand, London WC2R 0RL
A Penguin Random House Company

10 9 8 7 6 5 4 3 2 1
001-298134-March/17

marvel.com
© 2017 MARVEL

A CIP catalogue record for this book is available from the British Library.

ISBN: 978-0-24128-104-8

Printed and bound in China

www.dk.com

A WORLD OF IDEAS:
SEE ALL THERE IS TO KNOW

MEET THE GUARDIANS

A motley bunch of space adventurers has teamed up to protect the universe. They are the Guardians of the Galaxy! Each one has their own awesome skill or super-power, but together they are even mightier and can defeat any enemy.

STAR-LORD
Peter Quill is Star-Lord, the leader of the Guardians. He is brave and smart, and his team can always rely on him.

ROCKET RACCOON
Rocket Raccoon is a wisecracking weapons master. He is the only one who understands Groot, his best friend.

GROOT
Groot is a walking, talking alien tree. All he ever says is "I am Groot", but he is very powerful and can grow to huge sizes.

THE GUARDIANS' SHIP
The Guardians' lightning-fast starship is their mobile base. It doesn't have an official name, but Star-Lord calls it Cool Interstellar Travel Travelship!

INTERGALACTIC RESCUERS

The Guardians of the Galaxy may carry deadly weapons, but they also rely on brains, daring and, above all, teamwork.

DRAX THE DESTROYER

Drax was once a human called Arthur Douglas. Created to destroy the evil Thanos, this fierce, super-strong warrior found friendship with the Guardians.

GAMORA

Gamora is the fiercest woman in the universe. Raised by Thanos, she rejected his cruel ways and chose to fight on the side of good.

COSMIC CRUSADER

Peter Quill is Star-Lord, heroic leader of the Guardians of the Galaxy. Although born on Earth, he is half Spartoi (on his dad's side). He grew up to become the galaxy's greatest protector, and is known for being brave, adventurous and wild!

LEADER OF THE GUARDIANS
Star-Lord has led his team into – and out of – many dangerous situations. The Guardians don't always agree with him, but they trust him with their lives.

EMPEROR QUILL
After Star-Lord's father, J'Son, was overthrown as Spartoi Emperor, Peter was elected the new Emperor. Despite his best efforts, it turned out to be a job that did not really suit his free spirit.

EARLY YEARS
When Peter Quill was young, he dreamed of going into space. After becoming a NASA mechanic, he stole an alien ship that was being studied by scientists, and joyously set out for the stars.

EXPERT PILOT AND NAVIGATOR
Peter Quill was a natural pilot even before he became Star-Lord. Having spent years exploring the galaxy, he is now also a first-rate navigator.

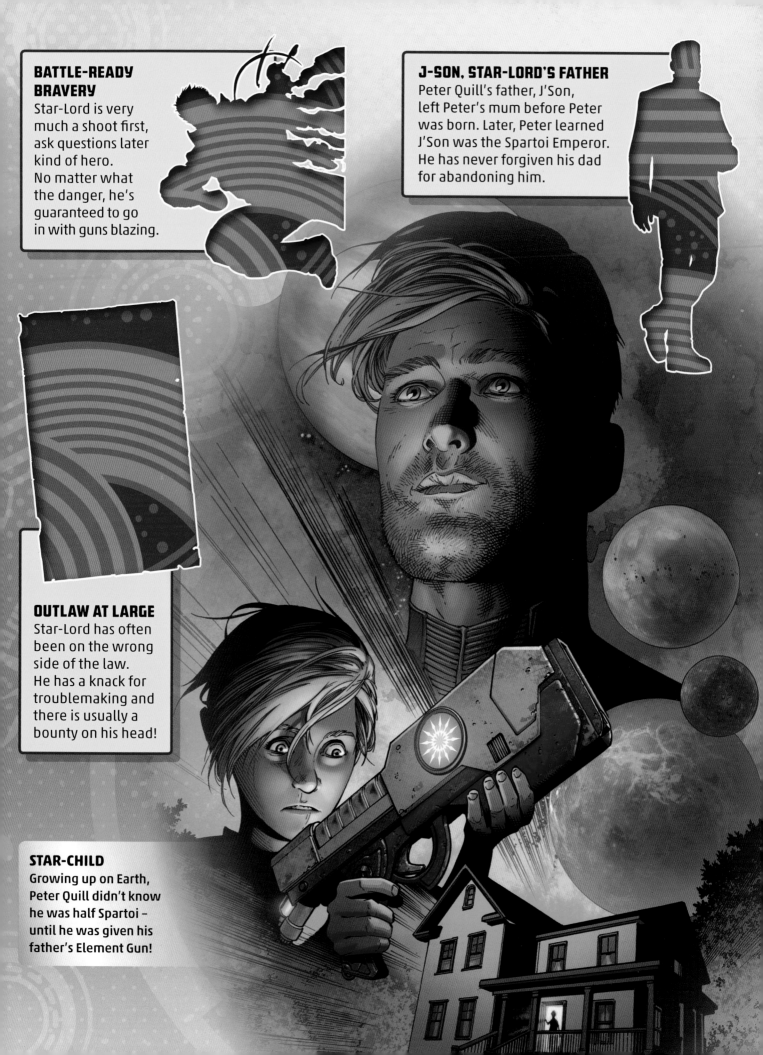

BATTLE-READY BRAVERY
Star-Lord is very much a shoot first, ask questions later kind of hero. No matter what the danger, he's guaranteed to go in with guns blazing.

J-SON, STAR-LORD'S FATHER
Peter Quill's father, J'Son, left Peter's mum before Peter was born. Later, Peter learned J'Son was the Spartoi Emperor. He has never forgiven his dad for abandoning him.

OUTLAW AT LARGE
Star-Lord has often been on the wrong side of the law. He has a knack for troublemaking and there is usually a bounty on his head!

STAR-CHILD
Growing up on Earth, Peter Quill didn't know he was half Spartoi – until he was given his father's Element Gun!

TEAM SPIRIT

The Guardians of the Galaxy are not just a team of heroes – they are friends as well. That friendship helps them work together during battles, and means that they can depend on each other in tough times. Their golden rule is: never leave a Guardian behind.

BEST BUDDIES

The first time Rocket Raccoon and Groot met, Groot was amazed that Rocket could understand him. Groot gave Rocket a huge hug, and Rocket said he'd always be his best pal.

©2017 Marvel

A HELPING HAND

To get around, Rocket often rides on Groot's shoulder. However, whenever Groot gets chopped down to size, it's Rocket who gets to give his little friend a lift!

FIGHTING SIDE BY SIDE

The Guardians couldn't be more different. When they are together, their combined powers make them a lean, mean fighting team.

TO THE RESCUE

A Guardian never lets another Guardian down. Even a part-time team-member like Iron Man will fly to the rescue when his teammates are in trouble.

KARAOKE STARS

When the Guardians win a battle, they like to party – hard! Fighting evil is a serious business, but fun activities like singing karaoke really help them to unwind.

DRAX AND GAMORA

Drax and Gamora have known each other for a long time. They respect one another as warriors and they both hate Thanos. As Guardians, they have become good friends.

BIG CELEBRATION

The Guardians love to celebrate victories together. After Groot saved the team from Spartoi soldiers, his teammates raised a loud toast to their friend.

LIFE ON THE SHIP

The Guardians spend a lot of time on their ship, whizzing around the galaxy on missions. They eat, sleep and play on it. It's their home from home.

STAR WARRIORS

Ever since they first came together, the Guardians of the Galaxy have welcomed other heroes onto the team. Some have been friends. Others have been adventurers they have met on missions. All have brought special powers and abilities to the group.

PHYLA-VELL
Phyla-Vell is a brave alien warrior. For a time she possessed the energy-controlling powers of Quasar. Now she relies on her sword-fighting skills and strength.

MANTIS
The mysterious Mantis was raised by priests from another world. She was trained in martial arts and mind-reading. She can read the thoughts of her Guardian teammates and their enemies.

ADAM WARLOCK
Adam Warlock is a sorcerer who has cosmic powers. He joined the Guardians to defend the galaxy from destruction by monsters from other dimensions.

COSMO THE SPACE DOG

Cosmo was sent into outer space from Earth as an experiment. While in space he transformed into a super-smart mind reader. On Knowhere, the Guardians' base, Cosmo is the security chief.

PIP

A troll from the planet Laxidazia, Pip Gofern is Adam Warlock's friend and sidekick. He is crafty, surprisingly strong and can teleport himself and other people.

MOONDRAGON

Heather Douglas is Moondragon, the daughter of Drax. She grew up on Titan, Thanos' home world, where she studied martial arts and developed amazing mind powers!

JACK FLAG

Jack Harrison is a crime fighter from Earth and friend of the Avenger Captain America. He joined the Guardians after they rescued him from a deadly, prison-like dimension.

FEARSOME FOES

The Guardians of the Galaxy have sworn to defend the cosmos. Their good deeds, however, have made them many enemies. These evildoers lurk in every dark corner of space – and they have the Guardians in their sights!

EGO, THE LIVING PLANET

The galaxy is home to countless strange creatures. Strangest of them all is Ego, a boastful planet who can think and talk, and is always causing trouble!

THE COLLECTOR

Taneleer Tivan is one of the oldest villains in the universe. Incredibly powerful, he is totally obsessed with collecting anything valuable – from rare objects to unique people!

YOTAT

Yotat was once a thief and smuggler. He stole weird alien weapons from the Collector. They accidentally exploded, turning him into a super-strong menace.

RONAN THE ACCUSER

Ronan is one of the Kree Empire's mightiest warriors and a strict officer of the law. He is judge, jury and executioner, dealing rough justice to anyone he feels deserves it – even the Guardians.

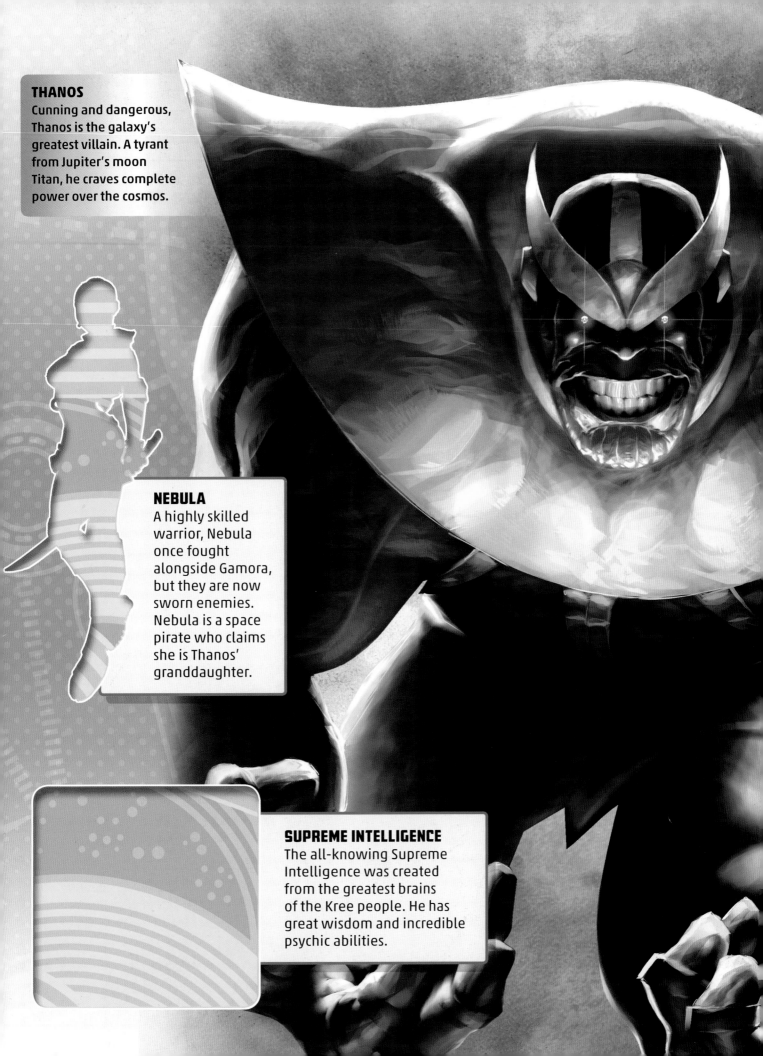

THANOS
Cunning and dangerous, Thanos is the galaxy's greatest villain. A tyrant from Jupiter's moon Titan, he craves complete power over the cosmos.

NEBULA
A highly skilled warrior, Nebula once fought alongside Gamora, but they are now sworn enemies. Nebula is a space pirate who claims she is Thanos' granddaughter.

SUPREME INTELLIGENCE
The all-knowing Supreme Intelligence was created from the greatest brains of the Kree people. He has great wisdom and incredible psychic abilities.

GALAXY QUEST
The Guardians have visited
many strange worlds, like
Hala, Spartax and Sacrosanct.
Now you can roam the galaxy
with your extra stickers!

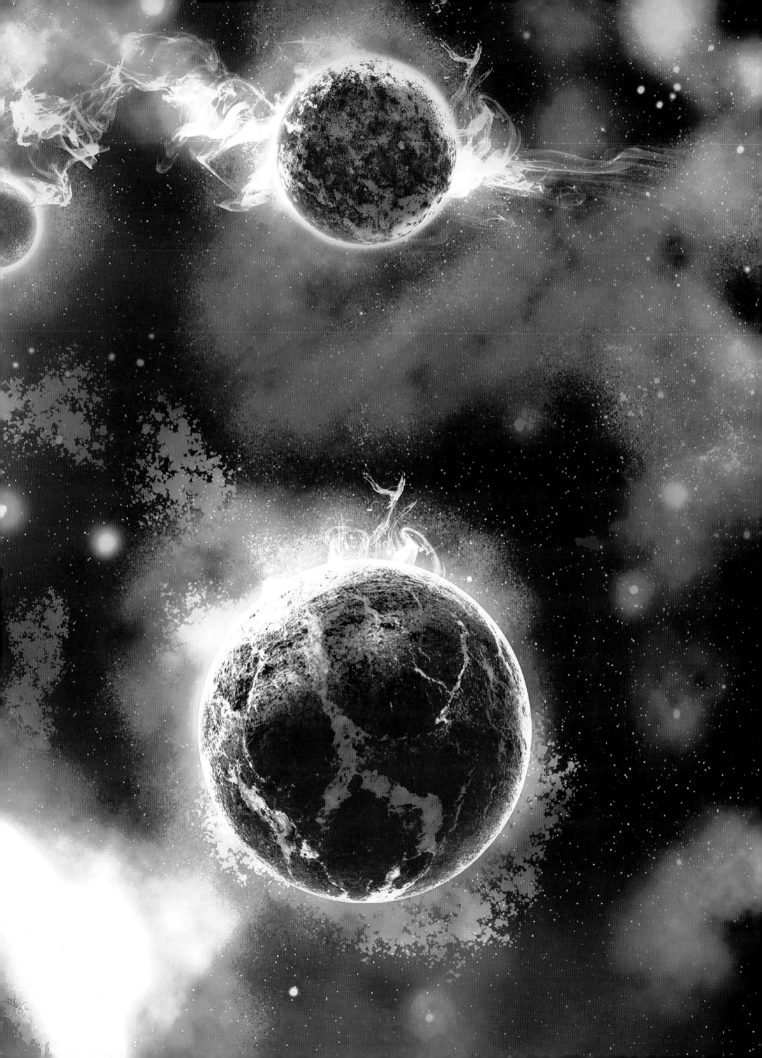

ADVENTURES IN OUTER SPACE

No mission is too perilous for the Guardians of the Galaxy. They will face any danger to keep their universe safe – and other universes, too. From extra-dimensional monsters to the ever-present menace of Thanos, the Guardians bravely meet any and all threats.

UNEASY ALLIES

To save the universe from an invasion by creatures from a demonic dimension, the Guardians teamed up with Thanos. They fought a Captain Marvel imposter and terrifying tentacled monsters.

SYMBIOTE TAKEOVER

Agent Venom's deadly alien symbiote can infect anyone. It once took control of the Guardians, including Rocket, to make them return it to its planet!

©2017 MARVEL

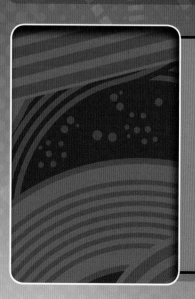

WAR OF KINGS

The Guardians had to split into two teams to try and stop a war between two galactic empires. Rocket's team boarded one of the warships to rescue an alien empress.

THROWDOWN WITH THANOS

Cut off from the other Guardians, Star-Lord and Nova were forced to fight Thanos on their own. They had to use Star-Lord's guns, Nova's powers and even a Cosmic Cube to defeat him!

LOST IN SPACE

Sometimes Rocket and Groot have their own adventures. Once, they got into a fight with some aliens. Their ship was destroyed and they wound up floating in space!

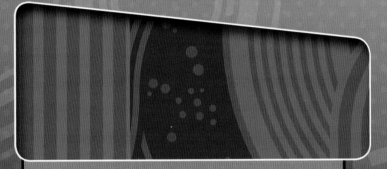

SECRET WARS

When the villainous Beyonders tried to destroy reality, the Guardians joined the fearsome fight to save Earth and the rest of the galaxy.

BATTLE FOR THE BLACK VORTEX

To stop the Black Vortex falling into enemy hands, Star-Lord almost let it transform him into a truly mighty being. However, he decided he couldn't trust himself with that much power.

DRAX AND THE DRAGON

On a solo mission, Drax ended up with an egg belonging to the dragon Fin Fang Foom. After it hatched, Drax had to protect the baby from other dragons!

THE FIRST MISSION

On the Guardians' first mission as a team, they fought the Universal Church of Truth and defeated a beast from another dimension!

SHOULDER TO SHOULDER

Some battles are too big for the Guardians of the Galaxy to handle alone. When they need help to battle godlike villains or repel a full-scale cosmic invasion, the Guardians call on friends and allies from Earth and beyond.

QUASAR

Wendell Vaughn is Quasar, protector of the Universe. He wears Quantum Bands on his wrists. These give him amazing cosmic energy powers.

CAPTAIN MARVEL AND ALPHA FLIGHT

Awesomely powerful, Carol Danvers, aka Captain Marvel, is an Avenger and a friend of the Guardians. She leads Alpha Flight – a band of Super Heroes that includes Aurora, Sasquatch and Puck.

NOVA

Teenager Sam Alexander is Earth's latest Nova, and he fights alongside the Guardians. Sam valiantly follows in the footsteps of his dad, Jesse, who was also in the Nova Corps.

THE AVENGERS
The Guardians can rely on the Avengers to help them battle the biggest villains of all. Their lineup includes some of the Earth's greatest heroes – Captain America, Iron Man, Thor and Hulk.

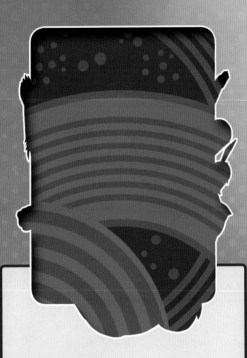

NOVA CORPS
The Nova Corps is the galaxy's police force. Its members are powered by the Nova Force, an unlimited source of energy. The most famous Nova is Earth's Richard Rider.

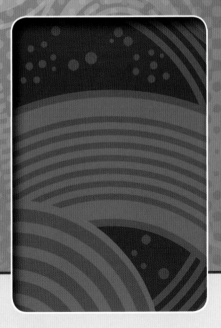

ROCKET AND GROOT
When they are not on missions with the other Guardians, best friends Rocket and Groot have their own adventures. Wherever they go, they have a habit of running into real trouble!

©2017 MARVEL

ANGELA
Like the Avenger Thor, Angela is a mighty Asgardian god. An expert swordswoman, she joined the Guardians for a time. Angela and her teammate Gamora respect each other as great warriors.

LUMINALS
The Luminals are a weird Avengers-like team from the planet Xarth III. These assorted aliens help protect the Guardians' base, Knowhere. They include Jarhead – a big brain in a rocket on robot legs!

THANOS, TERROR OF TITAN

Thanos is the ultimate big bad guy. An Eternal from the moon Titan, he is a cunning and cruel tyrant who wants to rule the galaxy. He is always looking for ways to increase his power. The only thing he loves more than conquest is Mistress Death.

EARTH IN HIS SIGHTS

From his throne on Titan, Thanos plots to take over Earth. However, the Guardians, the Avengers and other heroes stand ready to ruin his dark plans.

STAR-LORD VS THANOS

Star-Lord sees Thanos as the number one threat in the galaxy. He knows that the Guardians must defeat the mad Titan – no matter what the cost.

GAMORA'S FATHER

Gamora was adopted by Thanos when she was young. He trained her to be his weapon, but she grew up to hate her adoptive father.

DRAX VS THANOS
Drax was created by Thanos' father, Mentor, to destroy Thanos. The two enemies have fought many times. Drax has even managed to kill Thanos – although only temporarily.

©2017 MARVEL

MISTRESS DEATH
Thanos worships Mistress Death. She represents death in the universe. Thanos is so devoted to her that he once erased billions of beings across space!

POWER HUNGRY
Thanos is always on the hunt for objects of power. The Infinity Gems can change reality, especially when combined with the Infinity Gauntlet.

ALL-POWERFUL
Thanos is incredibly powerful, but he seeks other sources of power to add to his own. He once used a Cosmic Cube to turn himself into a god.

AWESOME OBJECTS

To help them in their missions, the Guardians of the Galaxy each have their own special weapons or equipment. But they'd better beware. The bad guys are always on the hunt for powerful objects and weapons to use against the heroes.

DRAX'S KNIVES
Drax tends to rely on his muscles in battle. But when his fists aren't enough, he carries a pair of super-sharp knives that he can quickly whip out.

INFINITY GAUNTLET
The Infinity Gauntlet was created by Thanos. He made it using the Infinity Gems – powerful jewels that allow the holder to control time, space, and reality.

BLACK VORTEX
This ancient mirror-like artifact must be handled with great caution. It transforms anyone who gazes into it, granting them enormous power. However, some people enjoy that power too much and end up misusing it.

STAR-LORD'S HELMET
Star-Lord can activate his alien helmet with a thought. The face mask allows him to breathe in space, and helps him to target enemies in battle.

STAR-LORD'S ELEMENT GUN

Star-Lord inherited the Element Gun from his father, J'Son. A Spartoi weapon, it can shoot energy blasts of any of the four elements: fire, air, water or earth.

ROCKET'S JETPACK AND BLASTER

Rocket really likes big blasters. They can be tricky to carry, though, so he sometimes uses a jetpack to get around.

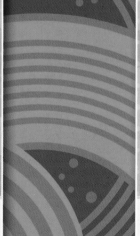

GAMORA'S SWORD

Trained by Thanos, Gamora is an expert with every type of weapon. Her favourite is her sword, Godslayer. Few can match Gamora's skill with a blade – except perhaps Angela.

PASSPORT BRACELETS

From their base, Knowhere, the Guardians sometimes use Passport Bracelets to get around. These watch-like devices let them teleport anywhere in any universe!

COSMIC CUBE

Cosmic Cubes are incredibly powerful weapons. They can destroy planets and change reality. Thanos wants to get his hands on one – and the Guardians want to stop him.

OUT OF KNOWHERE

The Guardians' huge headquarters, Knowhere, is home to many weird and wonderful aliens. Use your extra stickers to bring this amazing base to life.

ACROSS THE UNIVERSE

The Guardians of the Galaxy's missions take them all across space – and time. Some places, like Hala, they have visited often. Others, like the Planet of the Symbiotes, they've only explored once – which is more than enough!

PLANET OF THE SYMBIOTES
One of the weirdest places the Guardians have been is the Planet of the Symbiotes. A creepy, twisted world, Agent Venom's alien, shape-shifting suit comes from here.

KNOWHERE
Knowhere is the Guardians' home base. It is built inside the head of a Celestial – an ancient, godlike being. From here, the Guardians can teleport anywhere in the universe!

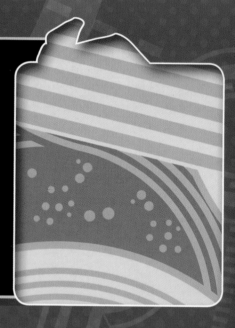

FUTURE AVENGERS MANSION
On a mission to the far future, the Guardians found that Earth had been destroyed. All that was left was the Avengers Mansion, floating in space!

HALA
The homeworld of the Kree, Hala is a place of high-tech wonders. Its fantastic cities are protected by giant robot sentries. Guardian Phyla-Vell comes from Hala.

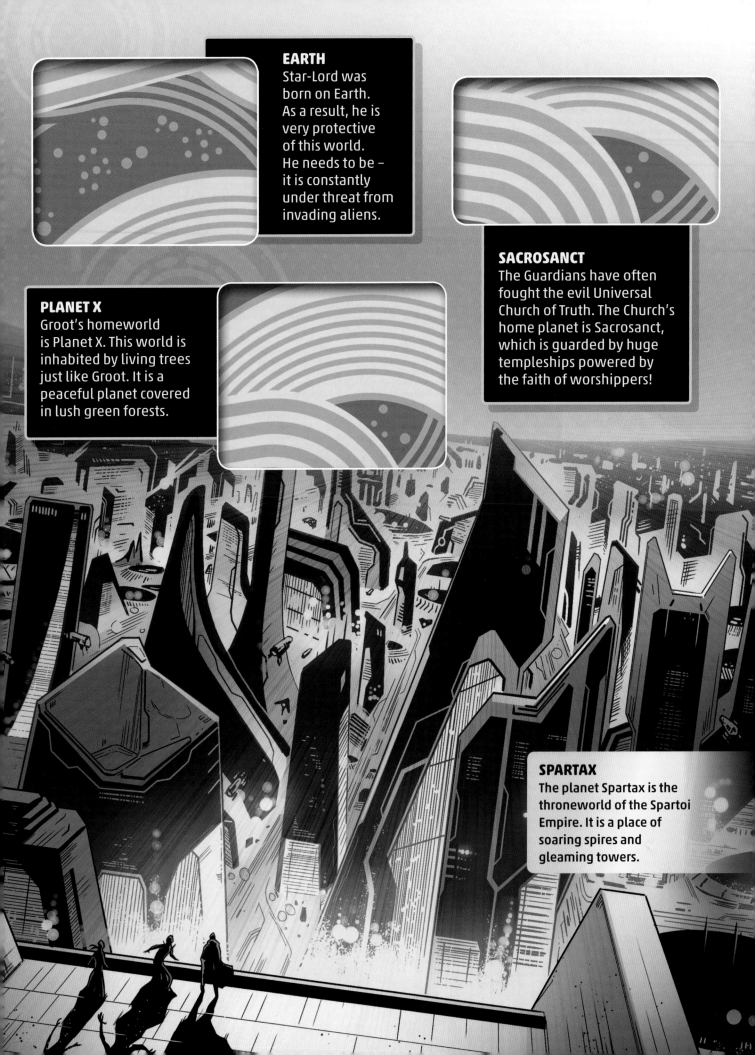

EARTH
Star-Lord was born on Earth. As a result, he is very protective of this world. He needs to be – it is constantly under threat from invading aliens.

SACROSANCT
The Guardians have often fought the evil Universal Church of Truth. The Church's home planet is Sacrosanct, which is guarded by huge templeships powered by the faith of worshippers!

PLANET X
Groot's homeworld is Planet X. This world is inhabited by living trees just like Groot. It is a peaceful planet covered in lush green forests.

SPARTAX
The planet Spartax is the throneworld of the Spartoi Empire. It is a place of soaring spires and gleaming towers.

GUARDIANS OF THE FUTURE

A thousand years in the future, Earth and its space colonies will be invaded by evil aliens. To fight these would be conquerors from outer space, a new Guardians of the Galaxy team comes together. These brave heroes watch over the 31st century!

MAJOR VICTORY
Major Victory is Vance Astro, an astronaut from our time who was frozen for 1,000 years. After he woke up, he formed the new Guardians of the Galaxy to battle Earth's alien invaders.

MARTINEX
Like all humans who live on Pluto, Martinex has a crystal-like body that helps him survive extreme temperatures. He can also project cold or heat rays.

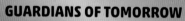

GUARDIANS OF TOMORROW
The future Guardians of the Galaxy come from different worlds where humans have settled. These Guardians united to protect humanity from evil alien rulers.

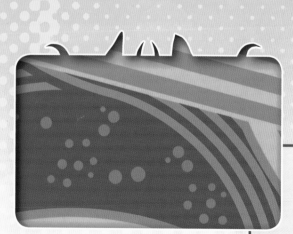

STARHAWK
Starhawk is a cosmic hero made up of two aliens: Stakar, a man, and Aleta, a woman. He can see the future – a very useful power for the Guardians!

CHARLIE-27
Charlie-27 comes from the human colony on the planet Jupiter. Living on this massive world has made him strong and powerful. He is the Guardians' strongman.

YONDU
On his planet, Centauri IV, Yondu was a skilled hunter. When his world was attacked, he joined the Guardians, using his lethal bow and arrow on the invaders!

NIKKI
Flame-haired and flame-powered – Nicholette Gold, aka Nikki, was raised on the planet Mercury. She was found by the Guardians after she escaped the alien conquerors.

GUARDIANS FACE-OFF
To save the 31st century from disaster, the future Guardians travelled back in time. There they met today's Guardians, who soon accused them of stealing their name!

AVENGERS ASSEMBLED

The Guardians are the galaxy's greatest protectors. The Avengers are Earth's mightiest heroes. When these two teams combine their power, they are an unstoppable force for good in the universe.

CAPTAIN MARVEL

Carol Danvers is Captain Marvel, one of the most powerful Avengers. Tough, fast and indestructible, she joined the Guardians after she rescued Star-Lord from a tight spot.

IRON MAN

An original Avenger, Tony Stark became a Guardian when he helped the cosmic heroes stop an attack on Earth. He has created special armour for space flight.

HEROES UNITED

The Guardians and the Avengers have matching skills. Drax and Hulk are amazingly strong, Gamora and Black Widow are superb fighters, and Star-Lord and Captain America are born leaders.

AGENT VENOM

After being injured in battle, Flash Thompson bonded with an alien shapeshifter and became Agent Venom. He represents the Avengers in the Guardians.

TITANIC TEAM-UPS

At first, the Avengers weren't sure what to make of the quirky Guardians. Star-Lord and his teammates soon earned their respect by battling Thanos and the evil Chitauri.

CELESTIALS

UNEASY ALLIES

BEST BUDDIES

NIKKI

EARTH IN HIS SIGHTS

ADAM WARLOCK'S MAGICAL POWERS

QUASAR

IRON MAN

PHYLA-VELL

INFINITY GAUNTLET

STAR-LORD

PLANET OF THE SYMBIOTES

EGO, THE LIVING PLANET

GAMORA'S MARTIAL ARTS

MAJOR VICTORY

FUTURE AVENGERS MANSION

THE COLLECTOR

GAMORA'S FATHER

EARLY YEARS

DRAX'S KNIVES

ROCKET RACCOON

MANTIS

CAPTAIN MARVEL AND ALPHA FLIGHT

A HELPING HAND

SYMBIOTE TAKEOVER

DRAX'S SUPERHUMAN STRENGTH

BUILDERS

GROOT

YOTAT

EMPEROR QUILL

KNOWHERE

MARTINEX

STAR-LORD VS THANOS

BLACK VORTEX

TO THE RESCUE

NOVA CORPS

CAPTAIN MARVEL

COSMO THE SPACE DOG

KREE

WAR OF KINGS

THE GUARDIANS'
SHIP

STAR-LORD'S HELMET

PIP

EXPERT PILOT AND NAVIGATOR

SPARTOI

DRAX VS THANOS

HALA

DRAX AND GAMORA

LUMINALS

RONAN THE ACCUSER

THROWDOWN WITH THANOS

STARHAWK

GROOT'S REGENERATING POWERS

ALL-POWERFUL

AGENT VENOM

PHYLA-VELL'S COSMIC POWERS

STAR-LORD'S ELEMENT GUN

ETERNALS

THE AVENGERS

DRAX THE DESTROYER

BATTLE-READY BRAVERY

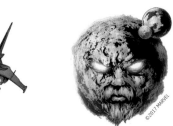

KARAOKE STARS

NEBULA

EARTH

MOONDRAGON

TITANIC TEAM-UPS

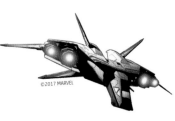

CHARLIE-27

GAMORA'S SWORD

JACK FLAG

ASGARDIANS

GAMORA

ROCKET AND GROOT

SACROSANCT

YONDU

OUTLAW AT LARGE

ROCKET'S COMBAT SMARTS

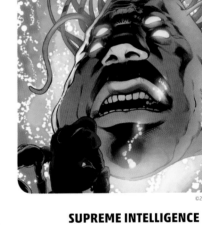

MISTRESS DEATH

SUPREME INTELLIGENCE

LIFE ON THE SHIP

LOST IN SPACE

EXTRA STICKERS

EXTRA STICKERS

EXTRA STICKERS

EXTRA STICKERS

EXTRA STICKERS

©2017 MARVEL

EXTRA STICKERS

©2017 MARVEL

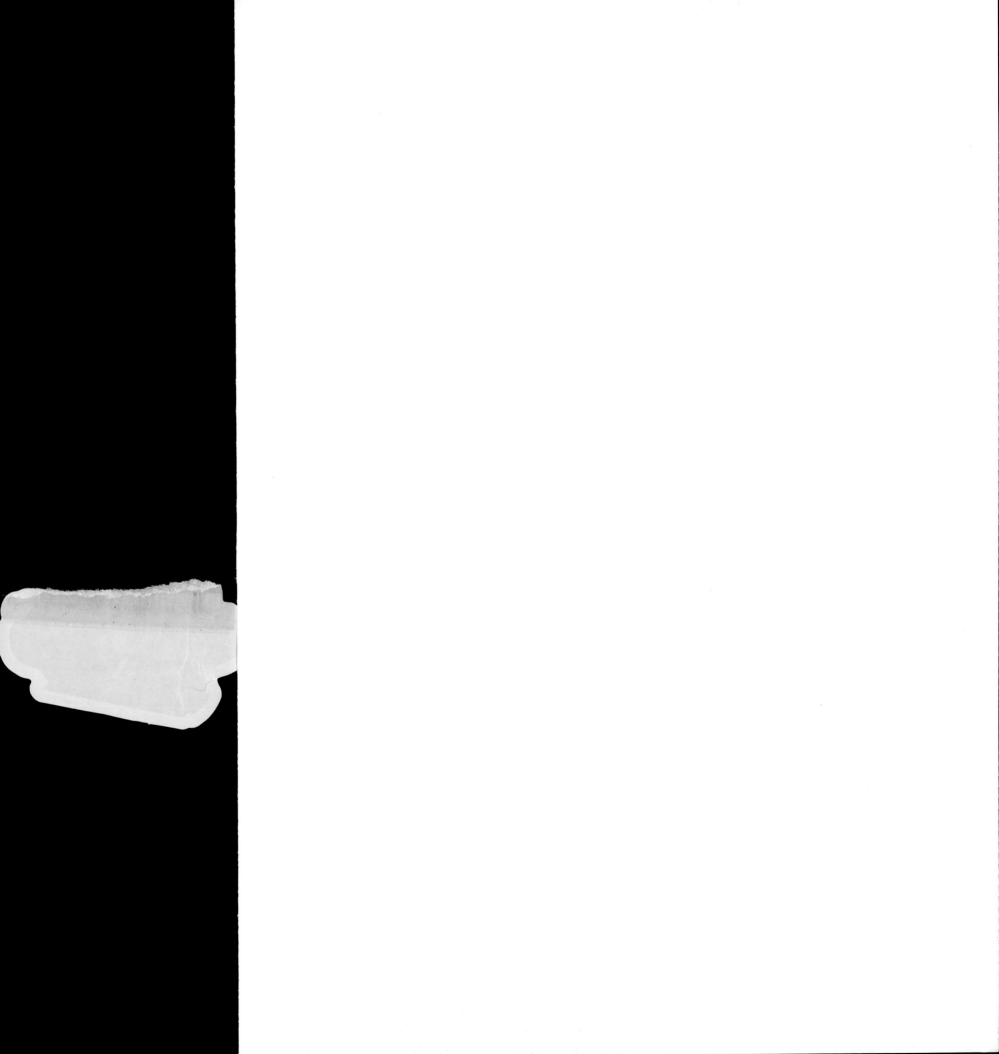

EXTRA STICKERS

EXTRA STICKERS

©2017 MARVEL

EXTRA STICKERS

EXTRA STICKERS

©2017 MARVEL

EXTRA STICKERS

©2017 MARVEL

EXTRA STICKERS

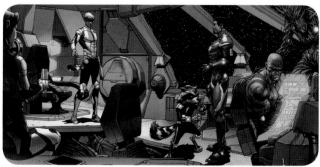

EXTRA STICKERS

EXTRA STICKERS

©2017 MARVEL

Meet the **cosmic outlaws** who have sworn to **protect** the galaxy at any cost.

Join **Star-Lord's** ragtag bunch of heroes, including **Drax, Gamora, Groot** and **Rocket Raccoon.**

Use the **extra stickers** to **create** your **own scenes.**

MARVEL
marvel.com
© 2017 MARVEL

DK
www.dk.com

£7.99

ISBN 978-0-2412-8104-8

9 780241 281048